The Red Pen

by Susan Hartley • illustrated by Anita DuFalla

Dan has a fat red pen.
Dan is on the mat
with the pen.

"Come here, Dan. Come get a hot bun," said Dad.

Dan ran to get a hot bun.
Tim ran to the red pen
on the mat.

"Dan, come have a nap,"
said Dad.
Dan ran to the bed
to have a nap.

Dan had a nap.
Dan did not see the red pen,
but Dad did!

"Tim," said Dad.

"You hid the pen!

You are a bad pup.

Here is the red pen, Dan."

Dan is on the mat
with the fat red pen.
Tim is on the mat
with the bun.